Poi Bowl

Dedications

To my Ama, Carolyn, one of the best party planners I know. Thank you for your help and support in writing my first book. Love you always and forever.

~ Jenna Hickman

For the amazing gifts in my life – My wife Grace and our boys Jamilo and Angelo. I love you guys!

~ A.V.

ISLAND HERITAGE™
PUBLISHING
A DIVISION OF THE MADDEN CORPORATION

94-411 Kōʻaki Street
Waipahu, Hawaiʻi 96797-2806
Orders: (800) 468-2800
Information: (808) 564-8800
Fax: (808) 564-8877
welcometotheislands.com

ISBN: 1-61710-361-6
First Edition, First Printing—2017
COP 170105

How about a
PINEAPPLE?

written by Jenna & Dani Hickman

illustrated by Antonio Verceluz

ISLAND HERITAGE™
PUBLISHING

We're going to have a party at the Purple Squid Café.
It's my best friend Nani's birthday that we celebrate today.
I picked a pineapple for her, but maybe it's not right.
I'll go remind our friends right now and ask for their insight.

2

3

Hello Mongoose! Don't forget,
Nani's birthday starts at four.
Is a pineapple a good gift, or
should I look some more?

Pineapples are pokey, but I have something grand.
I'll bring some fresh papayas, the sweetest in the land.
I don't know what to tell you,
so you'd best be on your way.
Why don't you go see Honu?
He'll have something good to say.

Good Day Honu! Don't forget, Nani's birthday starts at four.
Would you think a pineapple is a gift choice to explore?

6

Pineapples don't last long, but I made a gift that will.
Here's a seashell necklace.
THAT'S a present sure to thrill.
I don't have a clue what else Nani thinks is nice.
If you ask Pueo the Owl you'll get some
sound advice.

Hi Pueo! Don't forget, Nani's birthday starts at four.
Would a pineapple be a present she truly won't ignore?

Pineapples? Pineapples?
I eat dozens all year long.
For something special, COCONUTS!
There, you can't go wrong.
Coconuts are tough to beat,
of that I'm quite aware.
If you go visit Nene Goose,
she'll have a thought to share.

9

Greetings Nene! Don't forget,
Nani's birthday starts at four.
If she gets a pineapple, will she cheer or will
she snore?

Pineapples are fine, but a haku lei is awesome!
I worked very hard and hand-picked every lovely blossom.
Not much time to make a gift as wonderful as mine.
Maybe Mynah could help you find a present as divine.

11

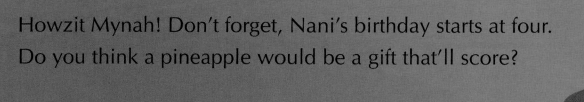

Howzit Mynah! Don't forget, Nani's birthday starts at four.
Do you think a pineapple would be a gift that'll score?

Giving gifts is not a game, please keep that in mind.
I'm picking juicy mangoes, as many as I can find.
The best things come from trees, but that may be hard for you.
You should go ask Gecko what exactly you should do.

13

14

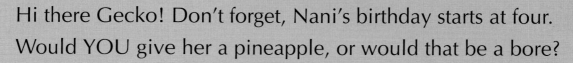

Hi there Gecko! Don't forget, Nani's birthday starts at four.
Would YOU give her a pineapple, or would that be a bore?

Do you think a pineapple is easy for one like me?
Hello!?! I'm a gecko! When I come, I'm bringing fresh lychee.
You're almost out of time, but don't give up on this just yet.
You could still ask Crab, but you know how grumpy
he can get.

Aloha Crab! Don't forget, Nani's birthday
starts at four.
Do you think a pineapple is an offering she'd adore?

Pineapples take too long to ripen,
and that's all I'll say on that.
I've already spent the last few days
weaving this lauhala hat.
There's no time to waste.
The party is where we need to go.
Help me and grab that bag.
Hurry up, you're moving way too slow.

16

The guests are here because it's almost four, and everything looks set.
But I'm still not sure a pineapple will be the safest bet.
I didn't get it from a tree. I didn't make it myself.
It's not from the deep blue sea, or the brightest thing on the shelf.
A pineapple it must be, though no one else did recommend.
Too late to second guess this, 'cause here comes Nani, my best friend.

20

NANI!

I'm so happy. Thanks for giving me what I wanted the most.
You threw me a festive party and you've been the perfect host.
Pineapples are my favorite and you gave me that one too.
Everyone is gathered here and it's all because of you.

21

It doesn't matter what you give, from flowers to fine art.
You never have to worry, if you give it from your heart.

23

the end